ROYAL BLOOD is an original publication of Avon Books.
This work has never before appeared in book form.

An Avon Illustrated Novel

AVON BOOKS
A division of
The Hearst Corporation
959 Eighth Avenue
New York, New York 10019

First Avon Printing, June, 1981

AN AVON ILLUSTRATED NOVEL

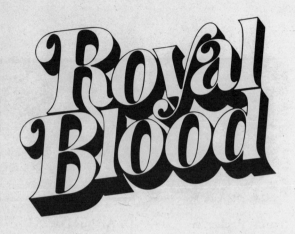

ALISSA CHANNING

◆ AVON
PUBLISHERS OF BARD, CAMELOT AND DISCUS BOOKS

Joanne Backer. A dedicated young nurse who chose a career in medicine and a lover who could never be her own.

Dr Arthur Day. A leading specialist in rare blood diseases. His wife's emotional problems and his demanding career are ruining their marriage.

Pauline Day. The Doctor's wife. Overshadowed by her husband's success, she is a prisoner of her own frustrations and disappointments.

Roberto D'Asturias. An arrogant Spanish nobleman who came to Dr Day for help and Joanne Backer for hope.

Joanne Backer is 25. Mature enough to take care of herself and strong enough to know she wants to work, learn, do a good job, and to fall in love.

THE MEDICAL

170

Joanne works in the MacDonald-Robbins Clinic, one of the most respected research and diagnostic centers in North America. Her intelligence and loyalty have made her an invaluable assistant to Dr Arthur Day.

Though only 34, Dr Day
is a world-renowned
expert in disorders and
diseases of the blood. He
has recently begun
treating private patients,
to put into practical
use the experience of his
brilliant research.

Joanne Backer has worked for 4 years as his research assistant and office nurse. Their relationship is based on friendship and respect, and their mutual dedication to their work. Their friendship has meant a great deal to Joanne over those years and has made her job even more rewarding.

Dr Day's exclusive practice is small but extremely busy, hardly leaving him time for his research. Each patient needs his special care and attention. Joanne worries a bit that the Doctor doesn't spend enough time at home.

If Joanne has a fault, it is that she often becomes too involved with the patients and their difficulties. Some patients are more demanding than others, and Joanne always responds to their problems. But her first loyalty is always to the Doctor and his needs. She tries to help him balance his own life.

Absorbed in her work,
Joanne didn't hear the
door open. A deep voice
startled her.

'I'm a very busy man.
When will the doctor be
free?'

'The Doctor is a busier man, sir.'

'Tell him Senor D'Asturias is ready to see him.'

'He'll see you when *he's* ready. Please be seated.'

Roberto D'Asturias wasn't used to being treated this way by a woman – even a very beautiful one. Still, coming from her...

'You may go in now, sir.'

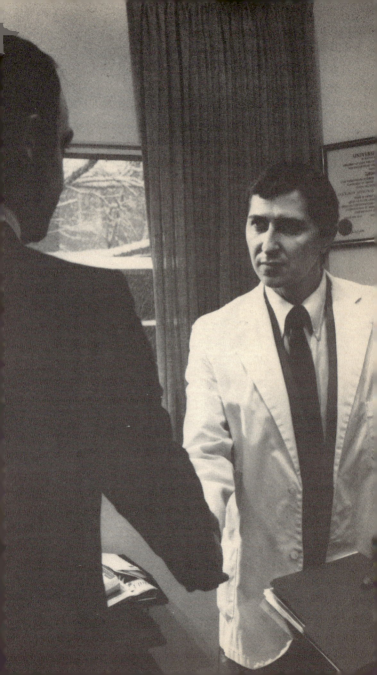

'So you're the famous
Dr Day...'

'Sorry to keep you
waiting. I understand
Dr Mancuso from the
Madrid Clinic sent you.
How is he?'

'He can't help me. He
says you can. I trust you
have all the details?'

'Yes I do. I'm sure you
understand how
unusual and serious
your case is... your
family background...'

'I know all of this, my father's funeral was just last month. Dr Mancuso has given me a melo-dramatic story. He said I have only months to live ... a man as young as I!'

'I'm afraid he may be right.'

'Don't be foolish. You must help me. I know that you will.'

'I'll do my best, Mr D'Asturias. Miss Backer will arrange a complete series of tests for you.'

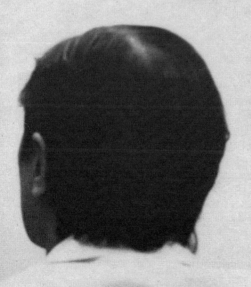

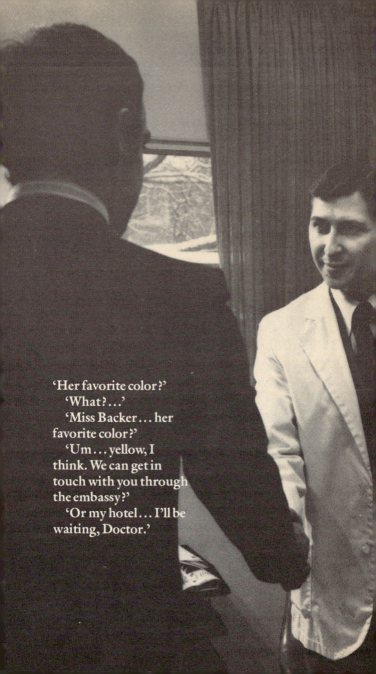

'Her favorite color?'
    'What?...'
    'Miss Backer... her
favorite color?'
    'Um... yellow, I
think. We can get in
touch with you through
the embassy?'
    'Or my hotel... I'll be
waiting, Doctor.'

When the patient reappeared, Joanne noticed how very handsome he was. And she noticed how much the tone of his voice had changed.

'Miss Backer, I must apologize for my rudeness when I came in, but my situation... my... no... It is inexcusable for a gentleman to act in such a manner... especially with such a beautiful lady as yourself.'

Caught by surprise, Joanne blushed but didn't respond. As he said goodbye and left, she watched the proud and graceful way he carried himself.

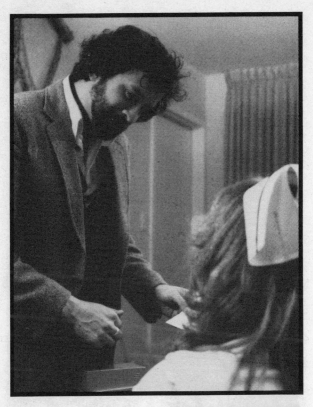

As the day rushed by,
patients came and went,
the Doctor's wife called
him several times, but
Joanne couldn't stop
thinking about the
elegant stranger ... and
how attractive he was.

All she learned from his file was his blood-type – rare – and that she was to arrange a set of even rarer tests for him. The Doctor was in no mood to answer her other questions. The calls from his wife seemed to have irritated him, as they often did.

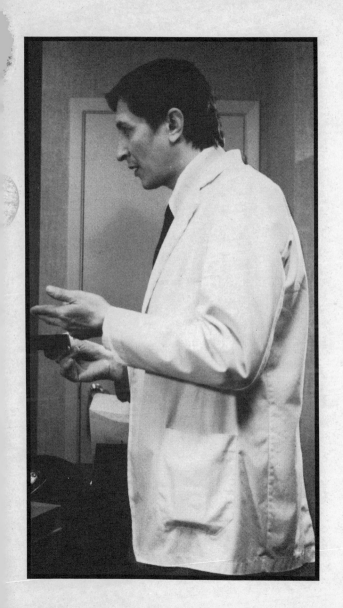

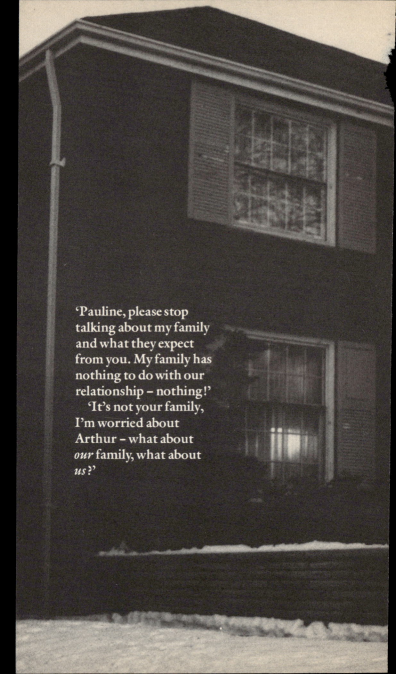

'Pauline, please stop talking about my family and what they expect from you. My family has nothing to do with our relationship – nothing!'

'It's not your family, I'm worried about Arthur – what about *our* family, what about *us*?'

Pauline Day had never felt welcome in the old Day mansion. Empty rooms echoed a past in which she had no part. She had always hoped that children would fill the house... and fulfill her marriage to Arthur, but now, recovering from a fallopian pregnancy, Pauline felt more alone than ever.

'Pauline. We may still have children. Don't you understand that I'm on your side?'

'But Arthur, I want you here. What you give me now isn't enough. It's not enough of you or your time.'

Pauline was close to tears.

'We need more than children to keep this marriage together. We need time together. I don't know what you do at that office but you're always there. There must be someone else. I know there's someone else.'

'Pauline, you're hysterical. There's no one.'

'No one...or do you mean nothing?'

Pauline wondered if there really was any hope left – for children, or for her marriage.

Dr Day, busy, tired Dr Day, wondered the same things.

Joanne was worried about the Days. She was afraid their personal problems were affecting the Doctor's work. She confided in a friend.

'I don't know, Carol ... it's just that each day he gets more and more difficult ... demanding ... he was never like this before.'

She was beginning to dread going to work. That feeling was completely new ... and she didn't like it at all.

But the next day started off perfectly, with a dozen yellow roses. Yellow roses. Joanne wondered who had sent them and why there was no card.

Since she wasn't seeing
anyone special, she
couldn't figure it out.
But the more she
thought, the more she
knew it was Arthur.

She knew she was right
when he asked her out
for lunch.

But they didn't speak of flowers.

'Joanne...listen... I...'

His pain was so obvious to her.

'Is it Pauline again?'

'She...she just isn't coming around after the operation; I've tried everything.'

'Everything but time, Arthur. You've been impatient these last few days. With me, with the patients, and I'm sure with Pauline.'

'She needs more from you Arthur. Are you sure you're really trying?'

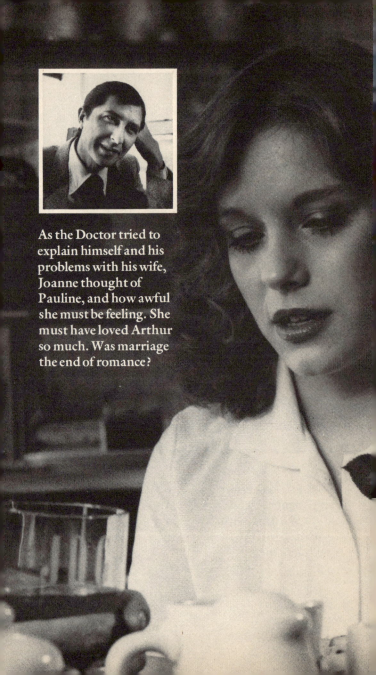

As the Doctor tried to explain himself and his problems with his wife, Joanne thought of Pauline, and how awful she must be feeling. She must have loved Arthur so much. Was marriage the end of romance?

Joanne also considered her own feelings for Arthur Day. She had always wished there was room in both their professional relationship and their friendship for something more. But she had always respected his marriage, and tried to help and understand when he seemed troubled. And now, his difficulties seemed more serious and more pressing.

'What beautiful flowers, Joanne. I do hope you enjoyed your lunch. I'm glad my husband thinks so highly of you. Arthur, I'd like to see you... privately.'

Joanne was quiet, knowing that anything she said would be a mistake.

'Pauline, this is no place to continue last night's discussion. You're not well or strong enough to be out. You should be…'

'Arthur, I've made a decision!'

'You're in no state to make any decisions. Now take these, go home and relax.'

'Arthur, you'll regret this.'

'We'll talk tonight, Pauline. At home.'

Arthur didn't know
why he acted as he did.
Perhaps talking to
Joanne made him realize
he had nothing to say to
his wife. He had nothing
to offer her except a
bottle of tranquilizers.

Pauline Day rushed out of the office with barely a glance at the handsome man who had just arrived.

As Roberto D'Asturias approached the desk, Joanne's problems, the Doctor's problems, his wife's problems, all disappeared as Joanne saw his smile.

'I hope you've had time to enjoy the flowers.'

'I didn't know...I mean...yes I have. Thank you.'

D'Asturias laughed gently. 'I'm the one who should be nervous. You're to take me to my tests, no?'

'I must thank you, Miss Backer, for gracing these trying days for me... with your beauty and charm.'

'Thank you... for the flowers... and...'

'I would much prefer to hear your thanks over dinner this evening.'

'But...'

Joanne was about to say no but she could find no reason to refuse. And she did want to know more about him.

'Joanne, I want you to know how important our patient is. Roberto D'Asturias is related to the Royal Family of Spain. He is unfortunately afflicted with a hereditary disease, one that has ravaged European royal families for centuries. I want to find a cure for that disease. For his sake... and for the sake of this medical center. Joanne, this could make history.'

Something had stirred in Joanne during the Doctor's revelations that afternoon. Was he throwing himself into the case to cure this strange disease? Or to avoid his own problems?

Either way, she knew he needed her help. And what of her feelings for Roberto D'Asturias?

Her life seemed so complicated all of a sudden.

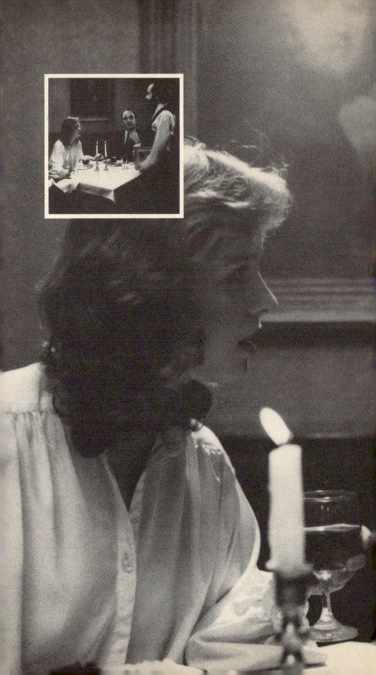

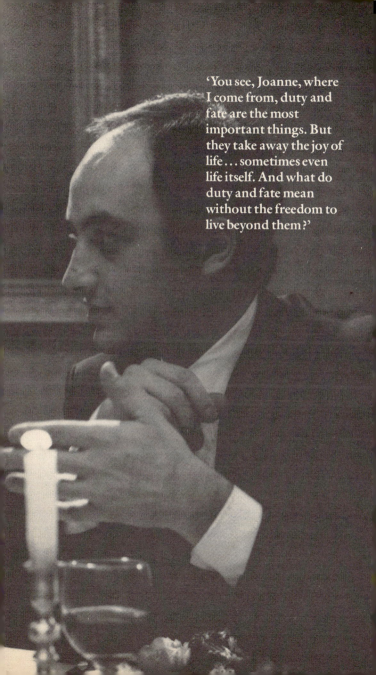

'You see, Joanne, where I come from, duty and fate are the most important things. But they take away the joy of life...sometimes even life itself. And what do duty and fate mean without the freedom to live beyond them?'

'But what about your
responsibility, your
family?'

'They mean less to me
than the feelings I am
beginning to have for
you.' Roberto laughed,
but Joanne could see his

nervousness. She couldn't help but think that there was something he wasn't telling her. It never crossed her mind that he was truly in love with her.

'Joanne, please come away with me. To New Orleans. To Carnival. There we will find life, there we will find love. A week, two weeks, not long for someone as young and beautiful as you. Will you come?'

'Roberto...I...'

But Joanne didn't answer. How could she?

'I know it seems such a short time for love to grow, Joanne, but it has. I love you...and this is the way of love, no?'

'The way of love?' Joanne smiled. He was so romantic.

'The ways of love are different for each and every one of us, Roberto. Thank you for the beautiful evening.'

'Goodnight, Miss Joanne Backer, goodnight. This has been the happiest night of my life.'

Joanne was wonderfully confused. Did she feel compassion for a sick but handsome man or was this the beginning of love?

'Goodnight, sweet senor, goodnight.'

Her dreams would be of Spanish castles and a handsome prince.

The next morning,
flowers. And the next.
On the third morning
more flowers and a note
begging her to come
with him to Carnival.
The days were a dream,
and the nights an agony
of indecision.

No one had ever
pursued her like this. It
was flattering, but con-
fusing at the same time.

'Dr Day, I've got to speak to you. Now. It's important.'

'Let's get through the day first, Joanne. We'll talk afterwards.'

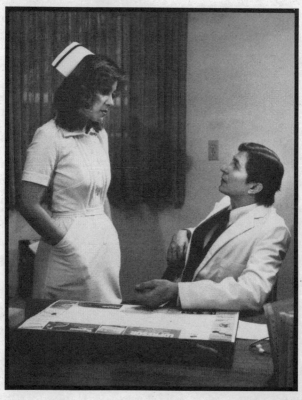

'Joanne, I don't know if you know, but Pauline's left me. Gone. For good. Two days ago. I feel guilty because I'm almost glad ...'

Joanne was torn. She was not surprised that Pauline was gone – that Arthur was alone. She had thought about it, considered it, and turned it over in her mind each night trying

to reach a decision about Roberto. But now she had made that decision.

'I'm leaving, Arthur. I want a leave of absence.' I'm sorry that it has to be now, but it has to be.'

Dr Day was astonished by Joanne's decision.

'But he's only got six months to live... he's leaving before the test results come back... before I can help him... before I... how can he be in love with you? How can you be sure with a man like that? I need you, Joanne, I need your help. I thought...'

'I'm sorry, Arthur.'

'Please, Joanne, think of what you're doing. Isn't there another way?'
'No…'

She would not change
her mind. Her heart left
her no choice.

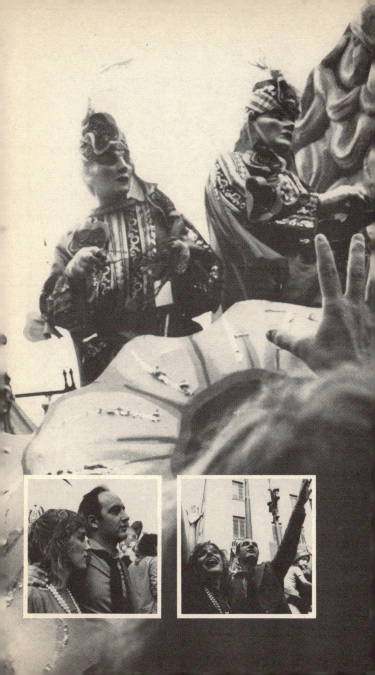

Joanne and Roberto
forgot everything in the
joy and life of Carnival.
They were falling in
love. It was even better
than it had been in her
dreams.

'...things a woman could only read about in books. A castle in Spain, servants, wealth, a life of ease... and perhaps a child to remember me by.

'Marry me Joanne, it would mean the world to me. I haven't long to be with you!'

'I know, Roberto.'
 'Then marry me and
make it forever.'
 'I know everything.'

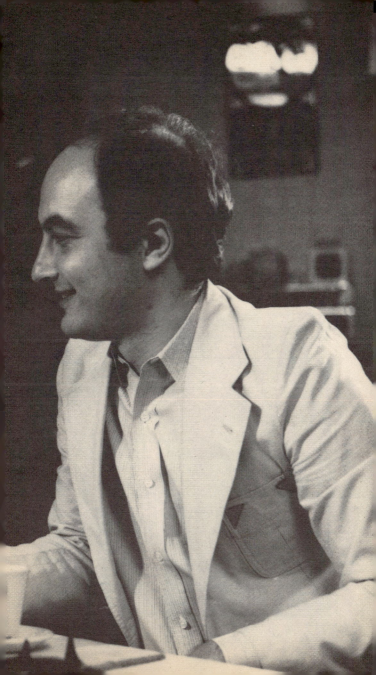

'...but right now...you must go back...back to Dr Day to try and cure you. That is the only important thing.'

'I can't think about marriage now, Roberto. Your life is worth more to me than . . . than a castle somewhere . . . than anything!'

But Roberto was no longer listening. He rose quietly and walked into the crowd.

Several minutes passed before Joanne realized he wasn't coming back.

Terrified, she rushed into the noisy street, her heart pounding. Where was he?

Joanne had to find Roberto. She had to explain. Explain that in all this crowd of people here, in the crush of humanity anywhere, he was the one she was looking for. He was the one, the only one she wanted.

She searched every-
where. Followed a hun-
dred different shadows,
a hundred different
Robertos, until she
realized she was alone in
the darkness. Alone and
afraid and lost.

Joanne finally returned to the hotel, hoping Roberto would be there, but all she found was a letter.

Joanne: Forgive me, I am a dying man. I love you, but have no right to steal the future from you. You must live your own life, and I, what remains of mine. You will not hear from me again. Su amor, Roberto.

JOANNE –
   Forgive me, I'm a o.....
MAN. I love you, but h....
RIGHT to steal the fu....
you. You must live yo....
life, and I, what h....
of mine. You will n....
me again.
                Su amor,
                   ROBERTO

So this was the way of love.

Doctor Day missed Joanne and he missed Pauline. With both of them gone it was a struggle to go on with his work.

But he had known when he chose to become a doctor that other people's problems, their illnesses, would have to come before his personal life if he was to be successful. And in the last week things had begun to come around, to seem somehow, easier.

Joanne had come back.

Without a word, without a scene.

With a smile, and hard work.

To the Doctor it seemed like no time had passed, just bad memories to be forgotten. To Joanne, it had all been a dream, as though it had happened to someone else, somewhere else, and a long long time ago.

One day she noticed a special obituary in the newspaper, notice of the death of Roberto D'Asturias, 'Prince of the Royal Blood,' and looked at the misty photograph of 'the ancestral home,' a home she might have shared with him if only she . . . if only he . . .

She knew the dream was over.

'Maybe I could have helped Roberto. I'm sorry, Joanne, truly sorry.'

I could have helped him too, thought Joanne, but he didn't want that.

Joanne Backer and Arthur Day had both gone through their own personal crises and come through them, ready to face together whatever the future held for them.

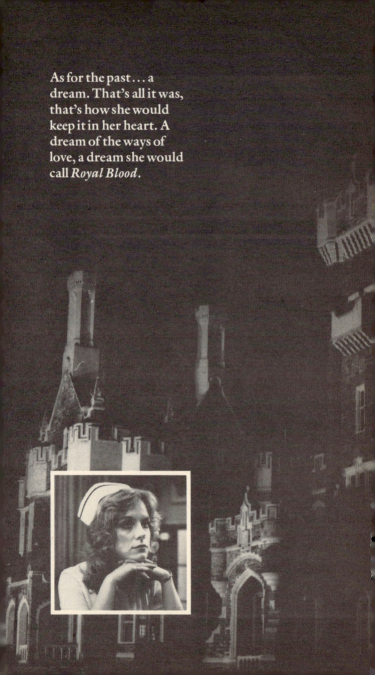

As for the past . . . a dream. That's all it was, that's how she would keep it in her heart. A dream of the ways of love, a dream she would call *Royal Blood*.

ROYAL BLOOD
ALISSA CHANNING

ROYAL BLOOD was photographed by Robert Holmes, directed by F. W. Taylor.

Production was coordinated by Janet Burke.

The characters were portrayed by Jorge de Medio, Sarah Hickling, G. Laight and Alvis Jarrett.

Made with the cooperation of The Brick Shirt House, Maryland Campbell, The Chelsea Inn (A Delta Hotel), Just Desserts, The Lafayette Medical Center, The Parson's Nose, The Prince Conti Hotel and Nancy Weber.

Shot on location in Toronto and New Orleans.